MEDITATION MANUAL

Based on the Buddha's Satipaṭṭhāna Sutta

MEDITATION MANUAL

Based on the Buddha's Satipaṭṭhāna Sutta

P.L. Dhar

EMBASSY BOOKS
www.embassybooks.in

MEDIDATION MANUAL
Based on the Buddha's Satipaṭṭhāna Sutta

First Edition 2017

Published in India by:
Embassy Book Distributors
120, Great Western Building,
Maharashtra Chamber of Commerce Lane,
Fort, Mumbai 400 023, India
Tel: (+9122) -30967415, 22819546
Email: info@embassybooks.in
www.embassybooks.in

Distribution Centres:
Mumbai, Bangalore, Kolkata,
Chennai, Hyderabad, New Delhi, Pune

ISBN: 978-93-86450-86-9

Page design and layout by PSV Kumarasamy

Contents

Preface 7

Introduction 11

A. Body

Breathing *17*
Postures *25*
Clear knowing *29*
Repulsiveness of the body *33*
Elements *37*
Nine Cemeteries *41*

B. Feelings 47

C. Mind 55

D. Dhammas

Hindrances *61*
Aggregates *69*
Sense Spheres *75*
Awakening Factors *85*
Noble Truths *93*

E. Conclusion 97

Preface

Satipaṭṭhānasuttaṃ is the basis of insight meditation practice in most traditions of Buddhism. Numerous books have been written expounding the methodology of meditation based on this discourse, the latest being the book by Ven. Analayo.

In these books the meditation instructions are embedded in scholarly exposition of the discourse and therefore very sparsely dispersed in the text. Here an attempt has been made to compile these instructions, mostly from the book by Ven. Analayo, along with the original text in Pali and its English translation. A few alterations have been done based on my own meditation practice and the advice given by other contemporary meditation masters like respected Goenkaji, Ajahn Sumedho, Rodney Smith, Ajahn Brahm, Joseph Goldstein, Ven. Vimalramsi and others.

Many a times a Pali word is interpreted differently by different meditation teachers and scholars leading to different practices. Rather than considering these as 'contradictory' and arguing which of them is correct, varied interpretations have been considered as 'expedient means' [*kusala upāya*] and attempt has been made to point out under what condition which interpretation is preferred.

I hope the compilation would be helpful in exposing the meditators to the nuances of various traditions and benefit from them.

Thanks are due to Prof. R.R.Gaur for organizing intensive discussions on this manual, and to Dr Rohi for converting the original document into an ebook.

Any suggestions for improvement would be deeply appreciated.

P.L.Dhar

Satipaṭṭhāna Sutta

This discourse, given at a town in North India called Kammāsadhamma, is one of the most important suttas in the Majjhima Nikāya. It gives practical guidance for cultivation of mindfulness and describes the four methods of steadfast mindfulness, namely, contemplating the body, contemplating sensation, contemplating the mind, and contemplating the mind-contents as the direct way for the purification of beings, for the overcoming of sorrow and lamentation, for the complete destruction of pain and distress, and for the attainment of nibbana.

This sutta appears in identical form in the Dīgha Nikāya with the 'saccapabbaṃ' in much greater detail.

Introduction

Pali text

Evaṃ me sutaṃ – ekaṃ samayaṃ bhagavā kurūsu viharati kammāsadhammaṃ nāma kurūnaṃ nigamo. Tatra kho bhagavā bhikkhū āmantesi – 'bhikkhavo'ti.

'Bhaddante'ti te bhikkhū bhagavato paccassosuṃ. Bhagavā etadavoca –

Uddeso

'Ekāyano ayaṃ, bhikkhave, maggo sattānaṃ visuddhiyā, sokaparidevānaṃ samatikk-amāya dukkhadomanassānaṃ atthaṅgamāya ñāyassa adhigamāya nibbānassa sacchikiriyāya, yadidaṃ cattāro satipaṭṭhānā.

'Katame cattāro?

Idha, bhikkhave, bhikkhu kāye kāyānupassī viharati ātāpī sampajāno satimā vineyya loke abhijjhādomanassaṃ, vedanāsu vedanānupassī viharati ātāpī sampajāno satimā, vineyya loke abhijjhādomanassaṃ, citte cittānupassī viharati ātāpī sampajāno satimā vineyya loke abhijjhādomanassaṃ, dhammesu dhammānupassī viharati ātāpī sampajāno satimā vineyya loke abhijjhādomanassaṃ.

English Translation

Thus have I heard.

On one occasion the Blessed One was staying in the Kuru country at a town of the Kurus called Kammasadhamma.

There the Blessed One addressed the monks, 'Monks.'

'Venerable Sir,' the monks replied.

The Blessed One said this:

[Exposition]

'Monks, this is the direct path for the purification of beings, for the overcoming of sorrow and lamentation, for the disappearance of *dukkha* and discontent, for the attainment of the right knowledge, and for the realization of *Nibbāna*—namely, the four *satipaṭṭhānas*.

Which four?

'Here monks, in regard to the body, a monk abides contemplating the body, diligent, clearly knowing and mindful — putting aside greed and discontent in regard to the world.

In regard to the feelings, he abides contemplating feelings, diligent, clearly knowing and mindful — putting aside greed and discontent in regard to the world.

In regard to the mind, he abides contemplating the mind, diligent, clearly knowing and mindful — putting aside greed and discontent in regard to the world.

In regard to the *dhammas,* he abides contemplating *dhammas*, diligent, clearly knowing and mindful — putting aside greed and discontent in regard to the world.

Meditation Instructions

[Background]

All the four *satipaṭṭhānas* need to be developed, even though one particular meditation practice can serve as the default object of attention.

The nearest translation of the term *cattāro satipaṭṭhānā* is fourfold establishing of awareness.

The term contemplating (*anupassati*) should be interpreted as understanding based on direct experience (awareness) of the nature of phenomena being observed.

Sati is neither mere attention nor just an intellectual analysis leading to some inference. At the mundane level, it is being aware of what one is doing; but its main aim is to penetrate into the real nature of what is observed.

The object of awareness – whether the body, breath, feelings, mind or *dhammas* – should be considered simply as perceived by the senses, without taking it to be 'I' or 'mine.' The meditator is then expected to intelligently process the input data gathered by mindful observations (*sampajāno satimā*) to unravel the real nature of the 'observed' – its impermanence, unsatisfactoriness, its impersonal nature – which is often concealed by appearances.

'Diligent' (*ātāpī)* implies attempting to maintain the continuity of practice, returning to the object of meditation at the earliest after the wandering of the mind. But this should be done keeping balance, 'putting aside greed and discontent' in regard to whatever is experienced.

Diligence arises from reflection on impermanence, law of karma, the preciousness of human birth and the suffering inherent in repeated rebirths.

Additional Remarks

[Background]

Commenatries advise that body and feeling contemplation could be the main practice for those who tend towards craving; meditators given to intellectual speculation should place more emphasis on contemplating the mind or *dhammas.*

Sampajānāti: clearly knowing

Satimā: mindful

sampajāno satimā: Mindful and clearly knowing

The central purpose of *satipaṭṭhānā* is to deconstruct the false notion of 'I' which arises due to identification with the body-mind complex. This is done by guiding the meditator through a series of contemplative investigations into the nature of body and mind, [the latter being further subdivided, on the basis of its functions, into four constituents, viz. feeling, perception, volition and consciousness] which reveal their impermamament and impersonal nature.

The last passage of this introduction prescribes the attitude with which the practice should be done.

A. Body - Breathing

Pali text

Kāyānupassanā ānāpānapabbaṃ

'Kathañca pana, bhikkhave, bhikkhu kāye kāyānupassī viharati? Idha, bhikkhave, bhikkhu araññagato vā rukkha-mūlagato vā suññāgāragato vā nisīdati pallaṅkaṃ ābhujitvā ujuṃ kāyaṃ paṇidhāya parimukhaṃ satiṃ upaṭṭhapetvā. So satova assasati, satova passasati. Dīghaṃ vā assasanto 'dīghaṃ assasāmī'ti pajānāti, dīghaṃ vā passasanto 'dīghaṃ passasāmī'ti pajānāti. Rassaṃ vā assasanto 'rassaṃ assasāmī'ti pajānāti, rassaṃ vā passasanto 'rassaṃ passasāmī'ti pajānāti. 'Sabbakāyapaṭisaṃvedī assasissāmī'ti sikkhati, 'sabbakāya-paṭisaṃvedī passasissāmī'ti sikkhati. 'Passambhayaṃ kāyasaṅkhāraṃ assasissāmī'ti sikkhati, 'passambhayaṃ kāyasaṅkhāraṃ passasissāmī'ti sikkhati.

'Seyyathāpi, bhikkhave, dakkho bhamakāro vā bhamakārantevāsī vā dīghaṃ vā añchanto 'dīghaṃ

añchāmī'ti pajānāti, rassaṃ vā añchanto 'rassaṃ añchāmī'ti pajānāti evameva kho, bhikkhave, bhikkhu dīghaṃ vā assasanto 'dīghaṃ assasāmī'ti pajānāti, dīghaṃ vā passasanto 'dīghaṃ passasāmī'ti pajānāti, rassaṃ vā assasanto 'rassaṃ assasāmī'ti pajānāti, rassaṃ vā passasanto 'rassaṃ passasāmī'ti pajānāti. 'Sabbakāyapaṭisaṃvedī assasissāmī'ti sikkhati, 'sabbakāyapaṭisaṃvedī passasissāmī'ti sikkhati, 'passambhayaṃ kāyasaṅkhāraṃ assasissāmī'ti sikkhati, 'passambhayaṃ kāyasaṅkhāraṃ passasissāmī'ti sikkhati.

Iti ajjhattaṃ vā kāye kāyānupassī viharati, bahiddhā vā kāye kāyānupassī viharati, ajjhattabahiddhā vā kāye kāyānupassī viharati. Samudayadhammānupassī vā kāyasmiṃ viharati, vayadhammānupassī vā kāyasmiṃ viharati, samudayavayadhammānupassī vā kāyasmiṃ viharati. 'Atthi kāyo'ti vā panassa sati paccupaṭṭhitā hoti yāvadeva ñāṇamattāya paṭissatimattāya anissito ca viharati, na ca kiñci loke upādiyati. Evampi kho, bhikkhave, bhikkhu kāye kāyānupassī viharati.

Ānāpānapabbaṃ niṭṭhitaṃ.

English Translation

[A. Body – Breathing]

'And monks, how does he in regard to the body abide contemplating the body?

'Here having gone to the forest, or to the root of a tree, or to an empty hut, he sits down; having folded his legs crosswise, set his body erect and establishing mindfulness in front of him, mindful he breathes in, mindful he breathes out.

'Breathing in long, he knows, long breath is inhaled [by me];' breathing out long, he knows, 'Long breath is exhaled [by me].'

Breathing in short, he knows, 'Short breath is inhaled [by me]; breathing out short, he knows, 'Short breath is exhaled [by me].'

He trains thus: 'I shall breathe in experiencing the entire body', he trains thus: 'I shall breathe out experiencing the entire body.'

He trains thus, 'I shall breathe in calming the bodily formation.' He trains thus, 'I shall breathe out calming the bodily formation.'

Just as a skilled turner or his apprentice, when making a long turn, knows, 'A long turn is made [by me],' or when making a short turn knows, 'A short turn is made [by me];' so too breathing in long, he knows, 'long breath is inhaled [by me]; or breathing out long, he knows, 'Long breath is exhaled [by me]'... He trains thus, 'I shall breathe in calming bodily formation.' He trains thus, 'I shall breathe out calming bodily formation.'

[Refrain]

'In this way, in regard to the body, he abides contemplating the body internally, or he abides contemplating the body externally, or he abides contemplating the body, both internally and externally. He abides contemplating the nature of arising in the body, or he abides contemplating the nature of passing away in the body or he abides contemplating the nature of both arising and passing away in the body. Mindfulness that 'there is body' is established in him to the extent necessary for bare knowledge and continuous mindfulness. And he abides independent, not clinging to anything in the world.

Bhikkhus, this is how in regard to the body, a monk abides contemplating the body.

End of breathing sub-section

Meditation Instructions

[Mindfulness of breathing]

The meditator should sit with legs crossed, back and neck straight but not tight, at an appropriate place with minimal disturbance. According to the instructions, the attention should be kept 'in front,' which could imply becoming aware of the breath wherever it is naturally felt in the body. However, it is helpful to confine the attention to an area around the nostrils and above the upper lip since focussing attention in a smaller area helps raise the level of concentration. The sensation of natural respiration, as the breath enters and leaves the nostrils, should be the object of awareness.

In case one has difficulty in feeling the breath in the nostrils area (one is not sure through which nostril it enters and leaves!) one can begin by just feeling the breath wherever it becomes effortlessly evident. Often it is the sensations felt in the chest area or even in the abdomen area. Slowly as the mind quietens down, it becomes possible to feel the breath around the nostrils and then one can rest the attention in this area. Ledi Sayadaw recommends for beginners counting of the breaths to focus the mind. Whenever the breath is not perceived counting is stopped and then restarted after its clear perception.

One can then begin investigating its nature – firstly, whether it is short or long; and thereafter become directly aware of its impermanent and impersonal nature – the breath going in, going in, stopping for a few moments, and then beginning its outward journey, coming out, coming out and then again stopping for a few moments, before it restarts (fortunately!). There is no one trying to breathe, it is happening naturally – just because there is life in the body – a very tenuous thread by which life is sustained.

One thus becomes effortlessly aware of the entire duration of in-breath and the out-breath.

As the mind quietens down it becomes possible to be aware of the whole body simultaneously with the awareness of the breath, as it comes in and goes out. If one notices any tension in any part of the body, the same is removed by relaxing the body.

Following the Ānāpānasatisutta, the word 'kāya' can also be interpreted as the 'body of breath'. This instruction thus means being constantly aware of the breath for its entire duration of inhalation and exhalation, as already mentioned above.

Whenever the mind wanders away, the attention should be brought back to the breath, not hurriedly, but after wilfully relaxing any tension created due to involuntary reaction to the same. This is of extreme importance for if the tension builds up, it would soon disturb the quietude of the mind.

The term 'calming the bodily formation' is also interpreted as calming the involuntary movement of the body in response to change in bodily sensations. This interpretation is the basis of the 'strong determination' meditation hours [adhiṭṭhāna] in Goenkaji's retreats. Following the Ānāpānasatisutta interpretation of the word 'kāya', and the definition of kāyasaṅkhāra as 'the in-breath and out-breath', Ven. Ledi Sayadaw interprets this instruction as "allaying and calming down the out-breath and in-breath". His advice: … If the breaths do not become automatically calmed down and allayed to the point of disappearance,…. then special additional endeavour must be made to make them gentler and gentler, and this must be pursued with resolution, not left unmindfully to take its own course.

Practising in this way one develops a balanced and detached attitude towards the body.

The instruction on 'contemplating the body externally' is best applied in daily life. Thus while interacting with people one can be aware of the 'body' of people with whom one in interacting. One could periodically direct the awareness towards the breathing of others by noticing the movement in the body wherever it is evident.

Additional Remarks

[Mindfulness of breathing]

The shifting of attention from abdomen to the chest and then to the entrance of nostrils, while 'feeling' the breath makes the object of attention progressively subtler and thus helps increase the level of concentration.

When practicing ānāpāna with a view to gain insight, one also notices the changing nature of the sensations associated with the respiration.

If the meditator notices that the mind is wandering away frequently, it is desirable to practice ānāpāna with a view to increase the concentration by focussing intently on an area around the nostrils, and taking a few deep or rapid breaths. If however one notices 'tension' arising due to too much effort, more spacious observation is helpful, i.e. noticing the breath wherever it is easily felt.

This last paragraph of the instructions - sometimes termed as the 'refrain,' occurs after each of the meditation exercises. It suggests (a) observing the phenomena arising in oneself and in others; (b) a shift of awareness from individual content of the experience to its general features viz. *anicca, dukkha* and *anatta,* i.e. its impermanence, unsatisfactoriness and impersonal nature. This is crucial for development of insight.

Relaxing helps accept the reality of wandering of mind. As the mind becomes tranquil it becomes evident: 'I' am not breathing- it is just happening.

This shifting of awareness between 'internal' and 'external' objects is helpful in achieving a skilful balance between 'introversion' and 'extroversion'; in removing boundaries between the 'internal' and the 'external', and in developing insight into the ever-changing and impersonal nature of the breathing process. This, of course, needs to be done cautiously lest it should appear like offensive gazing at the other person!

The last part of the refrain "*anissito ca viharati, na ca kiñci loke upādiyati*" suggests not considering anything in this world as "I" or "mine" and thus abiding free from dependence on anything.

The culmination of this practice is the realization: there is knowing and the object of knowing. There is no knower!!

Body - Postures

Pali text

Kāyānupassanā iriyāpathapabbaṃ

'Puna caparaṃ, bhikkhave, bhikkhu gacchanto vā 'gacchāmī'ti pajānāti, ṭhito vā 'ṭhitomhī'ti pajānāti, nisinno vā 'nisinnomhī'ti pajānāti, sayāno vā 'sayānomhī'ti pajānāti, yathā yathā vā panassa kāyo paṇihito hoti, tathā tathā naṃ pajānāti. Iti ajjhattaṃ vā kāye kāyānupassī viharati, bahiddhā vā kāye kāyānupassī viharati, ajjhattabahiddhā vā kāye kāyānupassī viharati. Samudayadhammānupassī vā kāyasmiṃ viharati, vayadhammānupassī vā kāyasmiṃ viharati, samudayavayadhammānupassī vā kāyasmiṃ viharati. 'Atthi kāyo'ti vā panassa sati paccupaṭṭhitā hoti yāvadeva ñāṇamattāya paṭissatimattāya anissito ca viharati, na ca kiñci loke upādiyati. Evampi kho, bhikkhave, bhikkhu kāye kāyānupassī viharati.

Iriyāpathapabbaṃ niṭṭhitaṃ.

English Translation

[Postures]

'Furthermore, when walking, the monk knows, 'I am walking.' When standing, he knows, 'I am standing.' When sitting, he knows, 'I am sitting.' When lying down, he knows, 'I am lying down.' Or however his body is disposed, he knows accordingly.

'In this way, in regard to the body, he abides contemplating the body internally, or he abides contemplating the body externally, or he abides contemplating the body both internally and externally. He abides contemplating the nature of arising in the body, or he abides contemplating the nature of passing away in the body or he abides contemplating the nature of both arising and passing away in the body. Mindfulness that 'there is body' is established in him to the extent necessary for bare knowledge and continuous mindfulness. And he abides independent, not clinging to anything in the world.

Bhikkhus, in this way too in regard to the body, a monk abides contemplating the body.

End of postures sub-section

Meditation Instructions

[Mindfulness in Various Postures]

These instructions advise the meditator to be aware of the body in a general manner, to be 'with' the body during its natural activities – sitting, standing, walking, and lying down – instead of being carried away by various thoughts and ideas.

In fact, for a beginner, it is easier to be aware of the body while sitting for meditation – noticing the sensations in the body wherever easily felt, e.g. the parts directly in touch with each other, the ground or the cushion, the movement of body due to breathing, tensions anywhere in the body due to taut posture (these should be relaxed) etc. – before beginning the practice of mindfulness of breathing.

Walking meditation can not only be practiced in daily life, but is also an integral part of formal meditation retreats. Often this is done by going around (or back-and-forth) an earmarked place in the retreat centre. One can be aware of the rapidly changing sensations as the feet touch the ground and are lifted up. Sensations in other parts of the body like legs, hands, etc., also influenced by the motion, can also be felt easily. One can also be aware of the changes in the mental states as one sees or smells different objects or hears different sounds. Keen observation of the movement of limbs during walking can lead to a peep into the impersonal nature of the body. Questions like: 'What is making the body to move?' 'Who is walking?' are helpful in developing this insight.

Additional Remarks

[Mindfulness in Various Postures]

Insight can be gained by noting that all minor postural adjustments are an impersonal response to the experience of physical pain inherent in having a body and experienced in all postures. Thus the insight into *anicca*, *dukkha* and *anatta* is developed.

These movements, when not observed, mask the *dukkha* inherent to the body.

Diligent practice of mindfulness in all the four postures reduces the mind's tendency to engage in digressive thoughts.

With sustained practice it becomes evident that the 'body' is moving due to the presence of consciousness and life force as modulated by the initial intention to walk. There is no 'I' who is doing the walking. The intention itself is a conditioned response to the unpleasant feeling or to some other perception [like walking is good for health], and even the perception is a result of some conditioning, and so on.

An important message from this section is that mindfulness should be maintained in all the postures. Walking meditation is thus as important as meditation in sitting posture. During formal retreats, when the sitting meditation sessions ends, the getting up from the cushion and walking out should be seen as a 'change of posture' and not a time for relaxing in mindlessness.

Body - Clear knowing

Pali text

Kāyānupassanā sampajānapabbaṃ

'Puna caparaṃ, bhikkhave, bhikkhu abhikkante paṭikkante sampajānakārī hoti, ālokite vilokite sampajānakārī hoti, samiñjite pasārite sampajānakārī hoti, saṅghāṭipattacīvaradhāraṇe sampajānakārī hoti, asite pīte khāyite sāyite sampajānakārī hoti, uccārapassāvakamme sampajānakārī hoti, gate ṭhite nisinne sutte jāgarite bhāsite tuṇhībhāve sampajānakārī hoti. Iti ajjhattaṃ vā...pe... evampi kho, bhikkhave, bhikkhu kāye kāyānupassī viharati.

Sampajānapabbaṃ niṭṭhitaṃ.

English Translation

[Clear Knowing]

'Again monks, when going forward and returning, he acts clearly knowing; when looking toward and looking away he acts clearly knowing…. when flexing and extending his limbs … when wearing the robes and carrying his outer robe and his bowl … when eating, drinking, chewing, and savouring… when urinating and defecating… when walking, standing, sitting, falling asleep, waking up, talking, and remaining silent, he acts clearly knowing.

'In this way, in regard to the body, he abides contemplating the body internally … externally … both internally and externally. He abides contemplating the nature of arising … of passing away … of both arising and passing away in the body. Mindfulness that 'there is body' is established in him to the extent necessary for bare knowledge and continuous mindfulness. And he abides independent, not clinging to anything in the world.

Bhikkhus, in this way too in regard to the body, a monk abides contemplating the body.

End of Clear Knowing sub-section

Meditation Instructions

[Mindfulness and 'Clear Knowing' while doing various activities]

The instructions given here can be applied both during formal retreats as also during daily life. Thus one should do all activities, say, for example, bathing, with full attention, keeping in mind the purpose of the action [to clean the body, and not to revel in pleasant sensations arising therefrom]; and its suitability [e.g.not bathing with cold water during viral fever]; being mindful of the changing postures and bodily sensations, and directing awareness to their impermanent and impersonal nature.

Sometimes *sampajāna* can reveal unwholesome motives hidden below apparent wholesome motivation while doing a wholesome act. This is a valuable insight which helps in purification of the mind.

Eating is one of the few activities in which all the five senses are engaged as one sees, smells, touches and tastes the food, and hears the sound produced while breaking or chewing it. Again this can be done with full awareness and *sampajāna*.

These instructions besides preventing the distraction of the mind help in developing a dignified and purposeful conduct with sense restraint, which facilitates development of insight into the true nature of reality.

This contemplation can also be done 'externally', i.e. while observing 'others' doing various activities.

Additional Remarks

[Mindfulness and 'Clear Knowing' while doing various activities]

The commentaries allude to four dimensions of clear knowing *(sampajāna)* for every activity, viz. the purpose (and the motivation); its suitability (appropriateness with respect to time, place and the effect on others); relationship to the meditation practice (i.e. doing all activities mindfully); and developing 'non- delusion' by clearly understanding the nature of reality (directly knowing through investigation: there is no doer of actions, only empty mind and matter phenomena happening).

These four dimensions of *sampajāna* are of great help in strengthening mindfulness and developing insight.

Mindful eating has been shown to be of great help in improving digestive health and reducing obesity. A Harvard study identifies seven practices of mindful eating:

https://www.youtube.com/watch?v=Emd9q6_o6Z0

Body - Repulsiveness of the Body

Pali text

Kāyānupassanā paṭikūlamanasikārapabbaṃ

'Puna caparaṃ, bhikkhave, bhikkhu imameva kāyaṃ uddhaṃ pādatalā adho kesamatthakā tacapariyantaṃ pūraṃ nānappakārassa asucino paccavekkhati – 'atthi imasmiṃ kāye kesā lomā nakhā dantā taco, maṃsaṃ nhāru aṭṭhi aṭṭhimiñjaṃ vakkaṃ, hadayaṃ yakanaṃ kilomakaṃ pihakaṃ papphāsaṃ, antaṃ antaguṇaṃ udariyaṃ karīsaṃ, pittaṃ semhaṃ pubbo lohitaṃ sedo medo, assu vasā kheḷo siṅghāṇikā lasikā mutta'nti.

'Seyyathāpi, bhikkhave, ubhatomukhā putoḷi pūrā nānāvihitassa dhaññassa, seyyathidaṃ sālīnaṃ vīhīnaṃ muggānaṃ māsānaṃ tilānaṃ taṇḍulānaṃ. Tamenaṃ cakkhumā puriso muñcitvā paccavekkheyya – 'ime sālī, ime vīhī ime muggā ime māsā ime tilā ime taṇḍulā'ti. Evameva kho, bhikkhave, bhikkhu imameva kāyaṃ uddhaṃ pādatalā adho kesamatthakā tacapariyantaṃ

pūraṃ nānappakārassa asucino paccavekkhati – 'atthi imasmiṃ kāye kesā lomā...pe... mutta'nti.

Iti ajjhattaṃ vā...pe... evampi kho, bhikkhave, bhikkhu kāye kāyānupassī viharati.

Paṭikūlamanasikārapabbaṃ niṭṭhitaṃ.

English Translation

[Body – Repulsiveness of the Body]

'Again, monks, a monk reviews the same body up from the soles of the feet and down from the top of the hair, enclosed by skin, as full of many kinds of impurities thus: 'in this body there are head – hairs, body-hairs, nails, teeth, skin, flesh, sinews, bones, bone marrow, kidneys, heart, liver, diaphragm, spleen, lungs, bowels, mesentery, contents of the stomach, faeces, bile, phlegm, pus, blood, sweat, fat, tears, grease, spittle, snot, oil of the joint and urine.'

'Just as though there were a bag with openings at both ends, full of various kinds of grain, such as hill rice, red rice, beans, peas, millet, and white rice, and a man with good eyesight were to open it and review thus 'This is hill rice, this is red rice,......this is white rice; so too he reviews this same body up from the soles of the feet and down from the top of the hair....... (as above)

'In this way, in regard to the body, he abides contemplating the body internally ... externally ... both internally and externally... contemplating the nature of arising ... of passing away … of both arising and passing away in the body. Mindfulness that 'there is body' is established in him to the extent necessary for bare knowledge and continuous mindfulness. And he abides independent, not clinging to anything in the world.

Bhikkhus, in this way too in regard to the body, a monk abides contemplating the body.

End of repulsiveness of the body sub-section

Meditation Instructions

[Contemplating Repulsiveness of the Body]

[Contemplating the Four Elements Constituting the Body]

[Contemplating on Corpses in Various Stages of Decay]

These three contemplations drive home the realization that one's own body and the bodies of others are inherently non-beautiful, impermanent and impersonal. It thus helps reduce one's tenacious attachment to the body. It has three facets entailing imaginative visualization, reflection and direct experience of bodily sensations.

While some parts of the body can be directly seen, others are not visible and can be visualized on the basis of anatomical knowledge, or even, in modern context, by seeing a video of the body's anatomy.

The simile of comparing this contemplation to examining a bag full of grains and beans suggests that just as examining these grains and beans will not stimulate any affective reaction, so the contemplation of various body parts should be done with a balanced and detached attitude.

Additional Remarks

[Repulsiveness of the Body]

This contemplation also reveals that what one calls as 'my body' is essentially an interdependent assembly of various parts, none of which can be really called as 'I' or 'mine'. Sister Vajira[1] sums this up precisely:

Just as when, with an assemblage of parts,
there's the word,
chariot,
even so when aggregates are present,
there's the convention of
living being.

The possibility of transplanting organs further 'confirms' this insight.

1 *http://www.accesstoinsight.org/tipitaka/sn/sn05/sn05.010.than.html*

Body – Elements

Pali text

Kāyānupassanā dhātumanasikārapabbaṃ

'Puna caparaṃ, bhikkhave, bhikkhu imameva kāyaṃ yathāṭhitaṃ yathāpaṇihitaṃ dhātuso paccavekkhati – 'atthi imasmiṃ kāye pathavīdhātu āpodhātu tejodhātu vāyodhātū'ti.

'Seyyathāpi, bhikkhave, dakkho goghātako vā goghātakantevāsī vā gāviṃ vadhitvā catumahāpathe bilaso vibhajitvā nisinno assa, evameva kho, bhikkhave, bhikkhu imameva kāyaṃ yathāṭhitaṃ yathāpaṇihitaṃ dhātuso paccavekkhati – 'atthi imasmiṃ kāye pathavīdhātu āpodhātu tejodhātu vāyodhātū'ti.

'Iti ajjhattaṃ vā kāye kāyānupassī viharati...pe... evampi kho, bhikkhave, bhikkhu kāye kāyānupassī viharati.

Dhātumanasikārapabbaṃ niṭṭhitaṃ.

English Translation

[Body – Elements]

'Again, monks, a monk reviews this same body, however it is placed, however it is disposed, as consisting of elements thus: 'in this body there are the earth element, the water element, the fire element, and the air element.'

'Just as though a skilled butcher or his apprentice, having killed a cow, would sit at a crossroads cutting it up into pieces; so too he reviews this same body…(continued as above)

'In this way, in regard to the body, he abides contemplating the body internally … externally … both internally and externally. He abides contemplating the nature of arising … of passing away … of both arising and passing away in the body. Mindfulness that 'there is body' is established in him to the extent necessary for bare knowledge and continuous mindful-ness. And he abides independent, not clinging to anything in the world. Bhikkhus, in this way too in regard to the body, a monk abides contemplating the body.

End of elements sub-section

Meditation Instructions

Contemplating Body – Elements

The four elements represent the basic qualities of matter that can be directly experienced by a meditator when he tries to 'feel' what is happening at various places in the body. These are solidity (or weightiness, heaviness or lightness), liquidity (or cohesion), airiness (or motion) and hotness or coldness (or temperature) all of which can be felt as bodily sensations during meditation.

During the body scan meditation as the meditator observes bodily sensations at various places the changing nature of elements becomes so clear. For example, the changes in sensations from heaviness to lightness to vibrations indicate the changing intensity of earth and air elements; the change in sensations from hot to cold indicates the change in the intensity of the fire element.

The effect of this particular meditation is illustrated with the simile of a butcher selling cow-meat indicating a shift in perception (*sañña*). He no longer perceives what he is selling as 'cow' but as 'meat'. Similarly, a shift in perception takes place when a meditator dissects the body into elemental qualities: the body is no longer experienced as 'I' or 'mine', but just a combination of these four qualities.

Sitting on a beach at noon, one can easily 'see' how the external world is also composed of these four elements.

This results in a healthy sense of detachment.

Additional Remarks

Contemplating Body – Elements

With sustained meditation on the bodily sensations, one can directly experience that the body, apparently so solid and compact, is essentially a flow of 'energy', with continuously deforming shape. The same is obviously true of the external world. Both are seen to be always in a state of vibration, without any essence. Insight of *anatta* is so evident then.

This meditation which helps in 'depersonalization' of the body is of great importance in the path of realization of the insight of *anatta* since it is through body that the world identifies us , and we can therefore easily fall in the trap of taking it as "I" or "mine".

However it is prudent to sound a note of caution. We should not become attached to this perspective of 'ultimate reality' prematurely, before we are truly free. A mere intellectual consent to the Truth - the body is empty, not me, not mine, just a bundle of waves - can trap us in neglecting the the 'apparent reality' of the body. Under the spell of this confusion, many senior meditators, and even meditation teachers, have committed unwholesome bodily deeds. A renowned Dzogchen master, Nyoshul Khen Rinpoche, warns about this attachement to emptiness in these words[2]:

Those who believe in *things* can be helped through various kinds of practice, through skillful means – but those who fall into the abyss of emptiness find it almost impossible to re-emerge, since there seem to be no handholds, no steps, no gradual progression, nothing to do.

---

2 *Quoted in "Mindfulness – a practical guide to awakening' by Joseph Goldstein, Sounds true publishers, Colarado, 2016, p 75*

Body – Nine Cemeteries

Pali text

Kāyānupassanā navasivathikapabbaṃ

'Puna caparaṃ, bhikkhave, bhikkhu seyyathāpi passeyya sarīraṃ sivathikāya chaḍḍitaṃ ekāhamataṃ vā dvīhamataṃ vā tīhamataṃ vā uddhumātakaṃ vinīlakaṃ vipubbakajātaṃ. So imameva kāyaṃ upasaṃharati – 'ayampi kho kāyo evaṃdhammo evaṃbhāvī evaṃanatīto'ti.

...pe... kākehi vā khajjamānaṃ kulalehi vā khajjamānaṃ gijjhehi vā khajjamānaṃ kaṅkehi vā khajjamānaṃ sunakhehi vā khajjamānaṃ byagghehi vā khajjamānaṃ dīpīhi vā khajjamānaṃ siṅgālehi vā khajjamānaṃ vividhehi vā pāṇakajātehi khajjamānaṃ....pe...

aṭṭhikasaṅkhalikaṃ samaṃsalohitaṃ nhārusambandhaṃ...pe... aṭṭhikasaṅkhalikaṃ nimaṃsalohita makkhitaṃ nhārusambandhaṃ... pe... aṭṭhikasaṅkhalikaṃ apagatamaṃsalohitaṃ nhārusambandhaṃ...pe... aṭṭhikāniapagatasambandhāni disā vidisā vikkhittāni, aññena hatthaṭṭhikaṃ ... pādaṭṭhikaṃ ... gopphakaṭṭhikaṃ ... jaṅghaṭṭhikaṃ... ūruṭṭhikaṃ ... kaṭiṭṭhikaṃ ...phāsukaṭṭhikaṃ ... piṭṭhiṭṭhikaṃ ... khandhaṭṭhikaṃ ... gīvaṭṭhikaṃ ... hanukaṭṭhikaṃ ...danta ṭṭhikaṃ ...sīsakaṭāhaṃ... pe...aṭṭhikāni setāni saṅkhavaṇṇapaṭibhāgāni...pe... aṭṭhikāni puñjakitāni terovassikāni ...pe... aṭṭhikāni pūtīni cuṇṇakajātāni. So imameva kāyaṃ upasaṃharati- 'ayampi kho kāyo evaṃdhammo evaṃbhāvī evaṃanatīto'ti ... kāye kāyānupassī viharati. Samudayadhammānupassī vā kāyasmiṃ viharati, vayadhammānupassī vā kāyasmiṃ viharati, samudayavayadhammānupassī vā kāyasmiṃ viharati. 'Atthi kāyo'ti vā panassa sati paccupaṭṭhitā hoti yāvadeva ñāṇamattāya paṭissatimattāya anissito ca viharati, na ca kiñci loke upādiyati. Evampi kho, bhikkhave, bhikkhu kāye kāyānupassī viharati.

Navasivathikapabbaṃ niṭṭhitaṃ.

Cuddasa kāyānupassanā niṭṭhitā.

English Translation

[Body – Nine Cemeteries]

'Again, monks, as though a monk were to see a corpse cast away in a charnel ground — one day, two days, three days dead — bloated, livid, and oozing matter…being devoured by crows, hawks, vultures, dogs, jackals, or various kinds of worms... a skeleton with flesh and blood, held together by sinews... a fleshless skeleton smeared with blood, held together by sinews... a skeleton without flesh or blood, held together by sinews... disconnected bones scattered in all directions... here a bone of the hand, there a bone of the foot… ankle,.. knee,.. thigh …pelvis… spine… back… shoulder… throat… chin,.. teeth… skull…. bones whitened, somewhat like the colour of shells... piled up, more than a year old... bones rotten and crumbling into a powder - he compares this same body with it thus: 'This body, too is of same nature, it will be like that, it is not exempt from that fate.'

'In this way, in regard to the body, he abides contemplating the body internally … externally … both internally and externally. He abides contemplating the nature of arising … of passing away … of both arising and passing away in the body. Mindfulness that 'there is body' is established in him to the extent necessary for bare knowledge and continuous mindfulness. And he abides independent, not clinging to anything in the world.

Bhikkhus, in this way too in regard to the body, a monk abides contemplating the body.

End of sub-section on nine cemeteries

End of all the fourteen body contemplations

Meditation Instructions

[Body – Nine Cemeteries Meditation]

This is a very powerful contemplation for reducing attachment to body, and prepares one to die without wailing and lamenting, having 'understood' the inevitability of death.

One can practice it whenever one has to go to a crematorium or burial ground and see how the body of a loved one crumbles within a few hours into a heap of ambers and bones, or gets decomposed in the earth within a few weeks.

Applying the memory of the decomposing body to one's own body, reflecting that in future one's own body will undergo the same process of decay and decomposition helps reduce 'conceit'.

It can also be practiced by reflection and visualization based on the text. For example, recalling everyday the pithy words repeated after every contemplation of this section: '*ayampi kho kāyo evaṃdhammo evaṃbhāvī evaṃanatīto'ti* (This body, too is of same nature, it will be like that, it is not exempt from that fate) can shake us up from the slumber of heedlessness and create the zeal to work for liberation from the cycle of repeated birth and death.

These reflections would lead to the insight that there is nothing inherently beautiful in the body (apparent beauty is just an illusion created by careful 'treatment' of the skin); its nature is to slowly decay and eventually perish. This is true not only of the body of 'others' which I can often observe easily, but also the body that I call as 'mine'.

This leads to disenchantment and dispassion, which are the foundation stones of liberation.

Additional Remarks

Body – Nine Cemeteries Meditation

This exercise should be done with care, in moderation and with a balanced mind. It should not lead to aversion or depression.

Mindfulness of breathing also reveals the thin thread by which our life hangs as the breath stops for a few moments [both during inhaling and exhaling]. Some meditators even get frightened when they 'experience' this, afraid that it might stop for 'ever'. But this can also be converted into a recollection of inevitability of 'death' when the breath would actually stop forever.

Seeing the video of a post-mortem can also help reduce the attachment to the apparent beauty of the body – it becomes quite evident that there is nothing inherently beautiful in any part of the body and this helps counteract sensual desire. See, for example, the short video at:

http://www.youtube.com/watch?v=8H6wbWorDOw

Pausing to see the gory sight of an animal crushed on a highway, the various parts of its body flushed out on the road, can also strengthen the insight of non-beautiful nature of the body.

In Anguttara Nikāya, the Buddha advises five daily contemplations for all to reduce bodily and mental attachment:

'I am subject to aging, have not gone beyond aging'.

'I am subject to illness, have not gone beyond illness.'...

'I am subject to death, have not gone beyond death.'...

'I will grow different, separate from all that is dear and appealing to me.'...

'I am the owner of my actions, heir to my actions, born of my actions, related through my actions, and have my actions as my arbitrator. Whatever I do, for good or for evil, to that will I fall heir.'

http://www.accesstoinsight.org/tipitaka/an/an05/an05.057.than.html

B. Feelings

Pali text

Vedanānupassanā

'Kathañca pana, bhikkhave, bhikkhu vedanāsu vedanānupassī viharati? Idha, bhikkhave, bhikkhu sukhaṃ vā vedanaṃ vedayamāno 'sukhaṃ vedanaṃ vedayāmī'ti pajānāti. Dukkhaṃ vā vedanaṃ vedayamāno 'dukkhaṃ vedanaṃ vedayāmī'ti pajānāti. Adukkhamasukhaṃ vā vedanaṃ vedayamāno 'adukkhamasukhaṃ vedanaṃ vedayāmī'ti pajānāti.

Sāmisaṃ vā sukhaṃ vedanaṃ vedayamāno 'sāmisaṃ sukhaṃ vedanaṃ vedayāmī'ti pajānāti, nirāmisaṃ vā sukhaṃ vedanaṃ vedayamāno 'nirāmisaṃ sukhaṃ vedanaṃ vedayāmī'ti pajānāti. Sāmisaṃ vā dukkhaṃ vedanaṃ vedayamāno 'sāmisaṃ dukkhaṃ vedanaṃ vedayāmī'ti pajānāti, nirāmisaṃ vā dukkhaṃ vedanaṃ vedayamāno 'nirāmisaṃ dukkhaṃ vedanaṃ vedayāmī'ti pajānāti. Sāmisaṃ vā adukkhamasukhaṃ vedanaṃ vedayamāno 'sāmisaṃ adukkhamasukhaṃ vedanaṃ vedayāmī'ti pajānāti, nirāmisaṃ vā adukkhamasukhaṃ vedanaṃ vedayamāno 'nirāmisaṃ adukkhamasukhaṃ vedanaṃ vedayāmī'ti pajānāti.

Iti ajjhattaṃ vā vedanāsu vedanānupassī viharati, bahiddhā vā vedanāsu vedanānupassī viharati, ajjhattabahiddhā vā vedanāsu vedanānupassī viharati. Samudayadhammānupassī vā vedanāsu viharati, vayadhammānupassī vā vedanāsu viharati, samudayavaya-dhammānupassī vā vedanāsu viharati. 'Atthi vedanā'ti vā panassa sati paccupaṭṭhitā hoti yāvadeva ñāṇamattāya paṭissatimattāya anissito ca viharati, na ca kiñci loke upādiyati. Evampi kho, bhikkhave, bhikkhu vedanāsu vedanānupassī viharati.

Vedanānupassanā niṭṭhitā.

English Translation

[B. Feelings]

'And how, monks, does a monk in regard to the feelings abide contemplating feelings?

When feeling a pleasant feeling, he knows, 'a pleasant feeling is experienced [by me];' when feeling an unpleasant feeling, he knows, 'an unpleasant feeling is experienced [by me];' when feeling a neither-painful-nor-pleasant feeling, he knows, 'a neither-painful-nor-pleasant feeling is experienced [by me].'

'When feeling a corporeal pleasant feeling, he knows, 'a corporeal pleasant feeling is experienced [by me].' When feeling a non-corporeal pleasant feeling, he knows, 'a non-corporeal pleasant feeling is experienced [by me].' When feeling a corporeal unpleasant feeling, he knows, 'a corporeal unpleasant feeling is experienced [by me].' When feeling a non-corporeal unpleasant feeling, he knows, 'A non-corporeal unpleasant feeling is experienced [by me].' When feeling a corporeal neither-painful-nor-pleasant feeling, he knows, 'A corporeal neither-painful-nor-pleasant feeling is experienced [by me].' When feeling a non-corporeal neither-painful-nor-pleasant feeling, he knows, 'a non-corporeal neither-painful-nor-pleasant feeling is experienced [by me].'

'In this way, in regard to the feelings he abides contemplating the feelings internally … externally … both internally and externally.

He abides contemplating the nature of arising … of passing away … of both arising and passing away in feelings.

Mindfulness that 'there is feeling' is established in him to the extent necessary for bare knowledge and continuous mindfulness. And he abides independent, not clinging to anything in the world.

Bhikkhus, in this way too in regard to the feelings a monk abides contemplating the feelings.

End of feelings section

Meditation Instructions

[Contemplating Feelings]

Feelings arise simultaneously with every act of cognition through any of the sense doors; i.e. whenever we see an object, or hear a sound, or smell a fragrance, etc. So this contemplation can be done on the basis of any of these feelings as these arise in our daily life. However, while meditating on a cushion with closed eyes, (as recommended by Sayagyi U Ba Khin) it is helpful to be primarily aware of the bodily feelings, i.e. 'feelings arising due to physical contact of touch (by way of friction, radiation and vibration of *kalapas* within) with the component parts of the body' since their impermanent nature is very evident which is helpful in developing the insight of *anicca*.

The systematic scanning of various body parts starting from the top of the head to the tip of the toes, [and in the reverse direction] as taught by Goenkaji, is very helpful *kusala upāya* for this contemplation.

The instructions given in the discourse indicate three dimensions of mindfulness. Firstly, to be aware of the feeling and its affective tone [practically speaking this implies periodically making a mental note] – i.e. whether these are pleasant, unpleasant or neutral, without reacting to these in any way. Secondly, we are advised to be aware of their impermanent nature. Thirdly, one should become clear through enquiry that there is no 'I' who is experiencing the feeling. It is a mental factor (*vedanā*) which arises along with cognition and experiences feeling, and another mental factor *sati* which knows 'feeling is being experienced'.

The awareness of sounds is another practice recommended by many teachers since the 'sounds' seem to be ever-present in the modern world. It entails being aware of the arising and passing away of sounds occurring naturally – e.g. due to passing vehicles, chirping of birds, rainfall, air-conditioner hum or people talking.

Senior meditators can also practice choiceless awareness, i.e. being effortlessly aware of whatever feeling arises in the body, [and through other sense doors] keeping breath as the default object of awareness.

While going for a morning walk, one can effortlessly be aware of the feelings, which arise on 'contact' at various sense doors – touch, sights, smells, sounds and the thoughts. Thus we can carry our 'object of meditation' seamlessly from cushion to daily life.

External contemplation of feelings and the state of mind (which is the next contemplation) of another person can be practised in daily life by 'inferring' about the same from their 'body language,' facial expression and the tone of voice. Patient non-reactive observation of the same would also reveal their impermanence.

Additional Remarks

[Contemplating Feelings]

Normally we react to pleasant feelings with craving and to unpleasant feelings with aversion, thus giving rise to *taṇha* which is the root cause of suffering. A mindful observer of the feelings, by the very fact of observation, no longer fully identifies with them or reacts to them, thus preventing the arising of *taṇha.* In case there is a reaction to a feeling, one notices that reaction as 'craving arising' or 'aversion arising' as the case may be, not taking even these reactions personally [see the next section *Cittānupassanā*].

Sustained contemplation of their ephemeral nature leads to disenchantment towards them. This strengthens dispassion, which is a prerequisite for liberation.

This practice can also help in maintaining equanimity in spite of painful bodily feelings arising in illness.

Questions such as 'who feels' force us to contemplate the feelings as just a mental factor and overcome the notion of 'self' that feels.

The practice of awareness of sounds strengthens our ability to pause before we respond to unpleasant words. Such pauses can prevent unconscious reaction, a frequent cause of misunderstanding in daily life.

The feelings that arise from 'contact' at any of the sense doors are called 'corporeal feelings'. Pleasant 'non-corporeal feeling' arise from wise sense restraint, seclusion, generosity, renunciation, concentration of mind, *brahma-vihāras* and insight; the unpleasant 'non-corporeal feeling' arise due to dissatisfaction with one's spiritual imperfections and disenchantment with worldly pursuits; and the neutral 'non-corporeal feeling' arise during deep equanimity experienced in *jhānas*.

Such 'external' contemplation can lead to an increasingly deeper appreciation of the temperament of others. Understanding its conditioned and 'non-self' nature can be very helpful in improving interpersonal relations. Thus mindfulness of the unpleasant feelings in others can help avoid automatic reaction of grief or cruelty; mindfulness of pleasant feeling can prevent jealousy and promote *mudita* (altruistic joy).

A caveat – 'clever' people can hide their true feelings!

C. Mind

Pali text

Cittānupassanā

'Kathañca pana, bhikkhave, bhikkhu citte cittānupassī viharati? Idha, bhikkhave, bhikkhu sarāgaṃ vā cittaṃ 'sarāgaṃ citta'nti pajānāti, vītarāgaṃ vā cittaṃ 'vītarāgaṃ citta'nti pajānāti. Sadosaṃ vā cittaṃ 'sadosaṃ citta'nti pajānāti, vītadosaṃ vā cittaṃ 'vītadosaṃ citta'nti pajānāti. Samohaṃ vā cittaṃ 'samohaṃ citta'nti pajānāti, vītamohaṃ vā cittaṃ 'vītamohaṃ citta'nti pajānāti.

Saṅkhittaṃ vā cittaṃ 'saṅkhittaṃ citta'nti pajānāti, vikkhittaṃ vā cittaṃ 'vikkhittaṃ citta'nti pajānāti. Mahaggataṃ vā cittaṃ 'mahaggataṃ citta'nti pajānāti, amahaggataṃ vā cittaṃ 'amahaggataṃ citta'nti pajānāti. Sauttaraṃ vā cittaṃ 'sauttaraṃ citta'nti pajānāti, anuttaraṃ vā cittaṃ 'anuttaraṃ citta'nti pajānāti. Samāhitaṃ vā cittaṃ 'samāhitaṃ citta'nti pajānāti, asamāhitaṃ vā cittaṃ 'asamāhitaṃ citta'nti pajānāti. Vimuttaṃ vā cittaṃ 'vimuttaṃ citta'nti pajānāti. Avimuttaṃ vā cittaṃ 'avimuttaṃ citta'nti pajānāti.

Iti ajjhattaṃ vā citte cittānupassī viharati, bahiddhā vā citte cittānupassī viharati, ajjhattabahiddhā vā citte cittānupassī viharati. Samudayadhammānupassī vā cittasmiṃ viharati, vayadhammānupassī vā cittasmiṃ viharati, samudayavayadhammānupassī vā cittasmiṃ viharati, 'atthi citta'nti vā panassa sati paccupaṭṭhitā hoti yāvadeva ñāṇamattāya paṭissatimattāya anissito ca viharati, na ca kiñci loke upādiyati. Evampi kho, bhikkhave, bhikkhu citte cittānupassī viharati.

Cittānupassanā niṭṭhitā.

English Translation

[C. Mind]

'And how, monks, does a monk in regard to the mind abide contemplating the mind? 'Here when the mind has passion, he knows the 'mind has passion,' and when the mind is without passion he knows 'the mind is without passion,' when the mind has aversion, he knows 'the mind has aversion' and when the mind is without aversion, he knows 'the mind is without aversion;' when the mind has delusion, he knows 'the mind has delusion' and when the mind is without delusion, he knows 'the mind is without delusion.'

'When the mind is collected, he knows 'the mind is collected' and when the mind is distracted, he knows 'the mind is distracted;' when the mind is expanded, he knows 'the mind is expanded' and when the mind is not expanded, he knows 'the mind is not expanded;'

when the mind is surpassable, he knows 'the mind is surpassable' and when the mind is unsurpassable, he knows 'the mind is unsurpassable.' When the mind is concentrated, he knows 'the mind is concentrated' and when the mind is not concentrated, he knows 'the mind is not concentrated;' when the mind is freed, he knows 'the mind is freed' and when the mind is not freed, he knows 'the mind is not freed.'

'In this way, in regard to the mind, he abides contemplating the mind internally ... externally ... both internally and externally. He abides contemplating the nature of arising ... of passing away ... of both arising and passing away in regard to the mind. Mindfulness that 'there is mind' is established in him to the extent necessary for bare knowledge and continuous mindfulness. And he abides independent, not clinging to anything in the world.

Bhikkhus, in this way too in regard to the mind a monk abides contemplating the mind.

End of the section on Mind

Meditation Instructions

[Contemplating the Mind]

The formal practice is usually done by choosing a default object of attention either breath or body-sensations, and periodically noting the state of mind. Whenever any unwholesome mental state arises – due to passion or aversion or delusion – a mental note is made of the same; and when that defilement ceases and the conjugate wholesome state - generosity or loving kindness or wisdom - arises, note is again made of the same.

The same attitude of calmly noting whatever is happening is adopted towards all other mental events like the distraction of the mind, and its getting focussed and various exalted states of mind achieved in *jhānas.*

This mental noting is helpful in strengthening mindfulness and identifying the conditions for arising and cessation of unwholesome states.

After sustained practice for a long time, it becomes possible to carry the same attitude into daily life making mental note of various emotions as they arise during worldly activities. The momentum of the practice enables one to pause for a few moments before responding to a situation, and to recall the impersonal nature of mental states. This helps avoid the tendency to disparage ourselves when unwholesome states arise and to exalt ourselves when wholesome states arise.

This pausing also prevents instinctive reactions governed by pleasure-pain principle, and gives an opportunity for the innate wisdom to influence the response to the situation.

One can become mindful of emotions arising in others through their body language, the change in their tone of voice, and their facial expressions. This facilitates the emergence of a more considerate response.

All the time the meditator should focus on the changeful nature of all the mental states including the peaceful states experienced in deep concentration. Thus the insights of *aniccā* are *anattā* are internalised as the conditional arising and cessation of the mental phenomena is seen objectively.

Additional Remarks

[Contemplating the Mind]

The term *citta*, translated here loosely as mind, refers to the mood or state of mind.

The practice aims at breaking our tenacious identification with thinking by training the mind to observe the mental events as mere objects and analyse them in terms of their qualitative features, without any reaction. Observing their changeful and conditioned nature breaks the stubborn habit of taking these states personally. The impersonal nature of thoughts becomes clear very soon when the meditator notices that it is not possible to have thoughts only as and when one would like to have them.

The instructions also tell us that the 'wandering of the mind' which is usually taken as a shortcoming in one's meditation, is just another state of citta to be observed!

It is important not only to note the presence of unwholesome states, but also their cessation. Gladness and joy arising from this cessation should not be glossed over, neither one should revel in it. This gladness gives confidence in the practice.

This discriminative observation also nurtures an intuitive ethical sensitivity, which helps as a reliable guide to proper conduct in life.

Elsewhere the Buddha suggests various strategies to overcome unwholesome states with effort.

http://www.accesstoinsight.org/lib/authors/soma/wheel021.html

In fact, this is one of the factors of the eightfold noble path – *samma vāyāma.*

http://www.accesstoinsight.org/ptf/dhamma/sacca/sacca4/samma-vayamo/

The above advice seems to be in disagreement with the instructions in the present Sutta of 'mere observation' of such states, letting these cease naturally. However, a study of other discourses reveals that the 'effort' is to be used as a last resort, in case of emergency when the intensity of the defilement is too strong to allow its 'mindful' observation and, if not checked, it may lead to unwholesome action.

Rodney Smith gives a deep insight into this practice: 'The Buddha is pointing to a deep acceptance of our humanity. He is saying that there is nothing wrong with us except our desire to be different. He is pointing back to self-formation and asking us to check our egos at the door. However, the mind is, let it be – we have no problem to overcome, no argument to cast, no side to take, no dispute to nourish, and no comparisons to make. All we can do is surrender our resistance and be completely self allowing.... The way to dissolve ourselves is through non-interference....'

D. Dhammas - Hindrances

Pali text

Dhammānupassanā nīvaraṇapabbaṃ

'Kathañca pana, bhikkhave, bhikkhu dhammesu dhammānupassī viharati? Idha, bhikkhave, bhikkhu dhammesu dhammānupassī viharati pañcasu nīvaraṇesu. Kathañca pana, bhikkhave, bhikkhu dhammesu dhammānupassī viharati pañcasu nīvaraṇesu?

'Idha, bhikkhave, bhikkhu santaṃ vā ajjhattaṃ kāmacchandaṃ 'atthi me ajjhattaṃ kāmacchando'ti pajānāti, asantaṃ vā ajjhattaṃ kāmacchandaṃ 'natthi me ajjhattaṃ kāmacchando'ti pajānāti, yathā ca anuppannassa kāmacchandassa uppādo hoti tañca pajānāti, yathā ca uppannassa kāmacchandassa pahānaṃ hoti tañca pajānāti, yathā ca pahīnassa kāmacchandassa āyatiṃ anuppādo hoti tañca pajānāti.

'Santaṃ vā ajjhattaṃ byāpādaṃ .... pe……..… yathā ca pahīnassa byāpādassa āyatiṃ anuppādo hoti tañca pajānāti.

'Santaṃ vā ajjhattaṃ thinamiddhaṃ.... pe ..., yathā ca pahīnassa thinamiddhassa āyatiṃ anuppādo hoti tañca pajānāti.

'Santaṃ vā ajjhattaṃ uddhaccakukkuccaṃ .... pe .... yathā ca pahīnassa uddhaccakukkuccassa āyatiṃ anuppādo hoti tañca pajānāti.

'Santaṃ vā ajjhattaṃ vicikicchaṃ ....pe .... yathā

ca pahīnāya vicikicchāya āyatiṃ anuppādo hoti tañca pajānāti.

'Iti ajjhattaṃ vā dhammesu dhammānupassī viharati .... bahiddhā vā .... ajjhattabahiddhā vā ...... samudayadhammānupassī vā .... vayadhammānupassī vā .... samudayavayadhammānupassī vā dhammesu viharati 'atthi dhammā'ti vā panassa sati paccupaṭṭhitā hoti yāvadeva ñāṇamattāya paṭissatimattāya anissito ca viharati, na ca kiñci loke upādiyati.

Evampi kho, bhikkhave, bhikkhu dhammesu dhammānupassī viharati pañcasu nīvaraṇesu.

Nīvaraṇapabbaṃ niṭṭhitaṃ.

English Translation

[D. Dhammas]

[Dhammas – Hindrances]

'And how, monks, does a monk in regard to the *dhammas* abide contemplating the *dhammas*?

[1] 'Here in regard to *dhammas,* he abides contemplating *dhammas* in terms of the five hindrances. And how does he in regard to the *dhammas* abide contemplating the dhammas in terms of five hindrances?

'If sensual desire is present in him, he knows 'there is sensual desire present within me;' if sensual desire is not present in him, he knows 'there is no sensual desire present within me;' and he knows how there is the arising of unarisen sensual desire, how arisen sensual desire can be abandoned, and how a future arising of the removed sensual desire can be prevented.

'If aversion is present in him, he knows … how a future arising of the removed aversion can be prevented.

'If sloth and torpor is present in him, he knows … and how a future arising of the removed sloth and torpor can be prevented.

If restlessness and worry is present in him, he knows … and how a future arising of the removed restlessness and worry can be prevented.

If doubt is present in him, he knows … and how a future arising of the removed doubt can be prevented.

In this way, in regard to the *dhammas* he abides contemplating the *dhammas* internally … externally … both internally and externally. He abides contemplating the nature of arising … of passing away … of both arising and passing away in regard to the *dhammas*.

Mindfulness that 'there are dhammas' is established in him to the extent necessary for bare knowledge and continuous mindfulness. And he abides independent, not clinging to anything in the world.

Bhikkhus, in this way too in regard to the *dhammas* a monk abides contemplating the *dhammas* in terms of the five hindrances.

End of the hindrances subsection

Meditation Instructions

Contemplation of Dhammas [Hindrances]

The practice of this contemplation is similar to that of the previous one, the focus being on the arising of mental factors that hinder the proper functioning of the mind. Learning to withstand the hindrances is therefore an important skill for progress on the path.

The Buddha groups these into five categories: sensual desire, aversion, sloth and torpor, restlessness and worry, and doubt; and they can be correlated with the mental states mentionedin the *Cittānupassanā* section above.

The contemplation of this section differs from that of *Cittānupassanā* in that not only does the meditator become objectively aware of the presence or absence of a hindrance, she is also advised to investigate to directly know the conditions that led to its arising, that assist in its removal and that prevent its future arising. This is especially important when one experiences a particular hindrance repeatedly for long time.

The most important reason for arising of various hindrances is unwise thoughts, for whatever one thinks frequently, that becomes the inclination of the mind. Thus constantly thinking about sensory pleasures is often the cause of arising of the first hindrance. Constantly complaining, thoughts of hurt caused (or may be caused) to ‘me’ or ‘mine’, or good done to ‘my’ enemy, condition the arising of the second hindrance of ‘aversion’.

Mindfulness, i.e. *sati*, is crucial for removing any hindrance since, without awareness of the presence or arising of a hindrance, little can be done about its removal or prevention. Often, just ‘seeing’ the presence of a hindrance is sufficient to weaken and eventually remove it. If mindfulness is weak, reflecting on the harmful consequences of the hindrance is also helpful in creating enthusiasm and energy to be more mindful and note the charcteristics of the hindrance very carefully. This requires patience and recalling the words of the Buddha, ‘patience is the highest austerity’, can be helpful in cultivating this quality.

Other factors more specific to each hindrance are enumerated in the next section.

A common factor in prevention of all the hindrances is engaging in suitable conversation with good friends and elders, and avoiding frivolous talk. Thorough study and reflection on the discourses with a view to gain clarity on the teachings is also useful, especially to prevent restlessness and worry, and doubt.

The whole exercise can also be done by inferring about the arising and passing away of the defilements in ‘others’ on the basis of their body language, tone of voice and facial expressions.

Additional Remarks

Contemplation of Dhammas [Hindrances]

The presence of sensual desire is similar to the arising of passion [of previous section]; the most common effect of presence of doubt is delusion [confusion], and the hindrances of sloth and torpor, restlessness and worry would certainly distract the mind.

Other suttas and the commentarial literature give some insight into the causes of arising, their cure and the prevention of arising of various hindrances.

Sensual desire

cause: Misperception that sensual pleasures will eventually make us happy, getting carried away by external 'beauty', especially of human body.

cure: *asubha-bhāvanā* i.e. contemplating on non-beautiful nature of body, on anatomical parts, on decaying corpse.

prevention: practice of sensory restraint, moderation in food, insight of *anicca.*

Aversion

cause: undue attention to irritating or repulsive features of a phenomenon, taking personally the phenomena (like criticism, failure, loss, blame etc.) which are impersonal.

cure: ignore negative qualities and pay attention to positive qualities of whoever or whatever is causing irritation.

prevention: five antidotes – developing *metta, karuna, upekha,* inattention, and reflecting on the principle of kamma.

Sloth and torpor

cause: discontent, boredom, laziness, drowsiness caused by overeating, depressed state of mind

cure: changing the meditation subject [from body to sight, sound, etc.], reflecting on and reciting a passage from the Buddha's teachings, opening eyes, pull one's ears, massage the body, get up, sprinkle water on eyes, look up the sky – cognition of light, walking meditation

prevention: reducing food intake, practising walking meditation

Restlessness and worry

cause: excessive energetic striving, focus on attaining and achieving, guilt and remorse, unwise attention to difficult worldly situations.

cure: relaxed attitude towards practice; use *ānāpāna* to still the mind, gladden the mind by reflecting on the merits acquired through the practice of *sīla*

prevention: ethical conduct, clarity about the teaching, good knowledge of discourses, avoiding provocative and prolonged discussions, wise reflection

Doubt:

cause: lack of clarity about the teaching, distinction between wholesome and unwholesome actions

cure and prevention: good knowledge of discourses and clarifying these through investigation and questioning, ethical conduct, strong commitment to practice

Dhammas – Aggregates

Pali text

Dhammānupassanā khandhapabbaṃ

383. 'Puna caparaṃ, bhikkhave, bhikkhu dhammesu dhammānupassī viharati pañcasu upādānakkhandhesu. Kathañca pana, bhikkhave, bhikkhu dhammesu dhammānupassī viharati pañcasu upādānakkhandhesu?

Idha, bhikkhave, bhikkhu – 'iti rūpaṃ, iti rūpassa samudayo, iti rūpassa atthaṅgamo; iti vedanā, iti vedanāya samudayo... atthaṅgamo; iti saññā.... iti saṅkhārā..... iti viññāṇaṃ, iti viññāṇassa samudayo, iti viññāṇassa atthaṅgamo'ti.

Iti ajjhattaṃ vā dhammesu dhammānupassī viharati, bahiddhā vā dhammesu dhammānupassī viharati, ajjhattabahiddhā vā dhammesu dhammānupassī viharati. Samudayadhammānupassī vā dhammesu viharati, vayadhammā-nupassī vā dhammesu viharati, samudayavayadhammānupassī vā dhammesu viharati. 'Atthi dhammā'ti vā panassa sati paccupaṭṭhitā hoti yāvadeva ñāṇamattāya paṭissatimattāya, anissito ca viharati, na ca kiñci loke upādiyati. Evampi kho, bhikkhave, bhikkhu dhammesu dhammānupassī viharati pañcasu upādānakkhandhesu.

Khandhapabbaṃ niṭṭhitaṃ.

Dhammānupassanā āyatanapabbaṃ

English Translation

[Dhammas – Aggregates]

Again, monks, in regard to *dhammas,* he abides contemplating *dhammas* in terms of the five aggregates of clinging. And how does he in regard to the *dhammas* abide contemplating the dhammas in terms of five aggregates of clinging?

Here Bhikkhus, a monk [knows]: 'Such is material form, such its arising, such its passing away; such is feeling, such its arising, such its passing away... Such is perception... Such are formations... Such is consciousness, such its arising, such its passing away.'

'In this way, in regard to the *dhammas,* he abides contemplating the *dhammas* internally … externally … both internally and externally. He abides contemplating the nature of arising … of passing away … of both arising and passing away in regard to the *dhammas*. Mindfulness that 'there are dhammas' is established in him to the extent necessary for bare knowledge and continuous mindfulness. And he abides independent, not clinging to anything in the world.

Bhikkhus, in this way too in regard to the *dhammas* a monk abides contemplating the *dhammas* in terms of the five aggregates of clinging.

End of the five aggregates sub-section.

Meditation Instructions

Contemplation of Dhammas [Aggregates]

The contemplation of all our subjective experiences in terms of the 'five aggregates of clinging' is the most direct approach to counter the illusion of personality. Close investigation reveals the conditioned nature of all the five aggregates (which can be viewed as the basic building blocks of our personality to which we are congenitally attached) thus undermining the basis on which conceit and 'I' or 'mine'-making take their stand.

In practical terms this contemplation can be undertaken – both during formal meditation and in daily life - by observing changes taking place in every aspect of one's personal experience, be these, for example, the cycle of breaths or the circulation of blood *(rūpa)*, the change of feeling *(vedanā)* from pleasant to unpleasant (and vice versa), the variety of perceptions *(saññā)* and volitional reactions *(saṅkhārā)* arising in the mind, or the changing nature of consciousness *(viññāṇa)*, arising at this or that sense door.

To give some more details through examples: by mindful observation of the breath or somatic sensations or sound, all of which belong to the aggregate of rūpa *(matter)*, one can recognize their arising and passing away, and learn: 'this is material form' arising and passing away incessantly, and so not personal, not belonging to me.

Similarly, by noting the arising and passing away of the aggregate 'feeling' [which feels] due to variety of incessantly changing sensations in the body, one appreciates the conditional, impermanent and impersonal nature of this aggregate. The same method can be applied in analysis of the other aggregates of perception, mental formation and consciousness.

This direct experience of the conditional, impermanent and impersonal nature of all aggregates leads to detachment from these constituent parts of one's personality which is a pre-requisite for breaking through the first fetter of *sakkāydiṭṭhi* or personality view.

Additional Remarks

Contemplation of Dhammas [Aggregates]

The first noble Truth summarizes the causes of *dukkha* as: 'briefly, the five aggregates of clinging are *dukkha*'.

Detachment from these five constituents of our subjective experience is thus a pre-requisite for complete cessation of *dukkha*.

First of these aggregates, material form refers to whatever is 'deformed' by external conditions such as cold, heat, hunger and thirst, mosquitoes and snakes etc. The subjective experience of the body is usually described in terms of the four elements which are constantly in flux, see *dhātumanasikārapabbaṃ* above. Still, inspite of repeated experience of the evanescent nature of form, a notion of solidity persists in our mind due to the usual description of body in terms of concepts –head, foot, leg, nose, ear etc. While all of them are constantly changing their designations remain constant. Caught in these unchanging concepts we fail to register the constant change in the body, creating a sense of identity with it. As Wittgenstein puts it: the sense of a separate self is only a shadow cast by grammar.

The next two in the sequence of aggregates are feeling (*vedanā*) and perception (*saññā*) which represent the affective and cognitive aspects of experience.

Perception refers to the act of identifying raw sensory data with the help of concepts or labels such as red, blue, man, woman, dog, car, bus , decent dress, good manners, nationalism, secularism, etc. It is conditioned by the upbringing, the familial, societal and religious values and conventions etc. and keeps changing in the light of education, interaction with the friends, and personal experience. Attachment to perception – "I am right!' syndrome – is often the cause of interpersonal conflicts.

The fourth aggregate comprises volitions (*saṅkhārā*) representing the conative aspect of the mind. The aggregate of volitions and intentions refers to the reactive or purposive aspect of the mind (like greed, anger, fear, envy, rapture, compassion etc.) and has a conditioning effect on all other aggregates. Volition itself is strongly conditioned by the ever changing perceptions and the state of mind.

The fifth aggregate is consciousness (*viññāṇa*), the act of being conscious of something, e.g. of form, sound, odur, etc. To recognise its conditioned and impersonal nature one needs to analyse the process of cognition. (See the 'Additional Remarks' in the next section on sense spheres).

This aggregate is prominently responsible for the notion of a substantial 'I' behind experience, the knower!

What we usually call a being is just a collection of these five aggregates which are constantly in a state of flux; birth and death are just their arising and passing away. There is no abiding Self in these. The Buddha explains this with telling similes in the Phena sutta : http://www.accesstoinsight.org/tipitaka/sn/sn22/sn22.095.than.html

Dhammas – Sense Spheres

Pali text

Dhammānupassanā āyatanapabbaṃ

'Puna caparaṃ, bhikkhave, bhikkhu dhammesu dhammānupassī viharati chasu ajjhattikabāhiresu āyatanesu. Kathañcapana, bhikkhave, bhikkhu dhammesu dhammānupassī viharati chasu ajjhattikabāhiresu āyatanesu?

'Idha, bhikkhave, bhikkhu cakkhuñca pajānāti, rūpe ca pajānāti, yañca tadubhayaṃ paṭicca uppajjati saṃyojanaṃ tañca pajānāti, yathā ca anuppannassa saṃyojanassa uppādo hoti tañca pajānāti, yathā ca uppannassa saṃyojanassa pahānaṃ hoti tañca pajānāti, yathā ca pahīnassa saṃyojanassa āyatiṃ anuppādo hoti tañca pajānāti.

'Sotañca pajānāti, sadde ca pajānāti, yañca tadubhayaṃ paṭicca uppajjati saṃyojanaṃ tañca pajānāti, yathā ca anuppannassa saṃyojanassa uppādo hoti tañca pajānāti, yathā ca uppannassa saṃyojanassa pahānaṃ

hoti tañca pajānāti, yathā ca pahīnassa saṃyojanassa āyatiṃ anuppādo hoti tañca pajānāti.

'Ghānañca pajānāti, gandhe ca pajānāti, yañca tadubhayaṃ paṭicca uppajjati saṃyojanaṃ tañca pajānāti, yathā ca anuppannassa saṃyojanassa uppādo hoti tañca pajānāti, yathā ca uppannassa saṃyojanassa pahānaṃ hoti tañca pajānāti, yathā ca pahīnassa saṃyojanassa āyatiṃ anuppādo hoti tañca pajānāti.

'Jivhañca pajānāti, rase ca pajānāti, yañca tadubhayaṃ paṭicca uppajjati saṃyojanaṃ tañca pajānāti, yathā ca anuppannassa saṃyojanassa uppādo hoti tañca pajānāti, yathā ca uppannassa saṃyojanassa pahānaṃ hoti tañca pajānāti, yathā ca pahīnassa saṃyojanassa āyatiṃ anuppādo hoti tañca pajānāti.

'Kāyañca pajānāti, phoṭṭhabbe ca pajānāti, yañca tadubhayaṃ paṭicca uppajjati saṃyojanaṃ tañca pajānāti, yathā ca anuppannassa saṃyojanassa uppādo hoti tañca pajānāti, yathā ca uppannassa saṃyojanassa pahānaṃ hoti tañca pajānāti, yathā ca pahīnassa saṃyojanassa āyatiṃ anuppādo hoti tañca pajānāti.

'Manañca pajānāti, dhamme ca pajānāti, yañca tadubhayaṃ paṭicca uppajjati saṃyojanaṃ tañca pajānāti, yathā ca anuppannassa saṃyojanassa uppādo hoti tañca pajānāti, yathā ca uppannassa saṃyojanassa pahānaṃ hoti tañca pajānāti, yathā ca pahīnassa saṃyojanassa āyatiṃ anuppādo hoti tañca pajānāti.

'Iti ajjhattaṃ vā dhammesu dhammānupassī viharati .... bahiddhā vā .... ajjhatta-bahiddhā vā ... samudaya-dhammānupassī vā ..... vayadhamm-ānupassī vā ..... samudayavaya-dhammānupassī vā dhammesu viharati.

'Atthi dhammā'ti vā panassa sati paccupaṭṭhitā hoti yāvadeva ñāṇamattāya paṭissatimattāya, anissito ca viharati, na ca kiñci loke upādiyati. Evampi kho, bhikkhave, bhikkhu dhammesu dhammānupassī viharati chasu ajjhattikabāhiresu āyatanesu.

Āyatanapabbaṃ niṭṭhitaṃ

English Translation

[Dhammas – Sense Spheres]

'Again, monks, in regard to *dhammas* a monk abides contemplating *dhammas* in terms of the six internal and external sense-spheres. And how does he in regard to the *dhammas* abide contemplating the dhammas in terms of the six internal and external sense-spheres?

'Here he knows the eye, he knows forms, and he knows the fetter that arises dependent on both. He knows how an unarisen fetter can arise, knows how an arisen fetter can be removed and how a future arising of the fetter that has been removed can be prevented.

'Here he knows the ear, he knows sounds, and he knows the fetter that arises dependent on both. He knows how an unarisen fetter can arise, knows how an arisen fetter can be removed and how a future arising of the fetter that has been removed can be prevented.

'Here he knows the nose, he knows odours, and he knows the fetter that arises dependent on both. He knows how an unarisen fetter can arise, knows how an arisen fetter can be removed and how a future arising of the fetter that has been removed can be prevented.

‘Here he knows the tongue, he knows flavours, and he knows the fetter that arises dependent on both. He knows how an unarisen fetter can arise, knows how an arisen fetter can be removed and how a future arising of the fetter that has been removed can be prevented.

‘Here he knows the body, he knows tangibles, and he knows the fetter that arises dependent on both. He knows how an unarisen fetter can arise, knows how an arisen fetter can be removed and how a future arising of the fetter that has been removed can be prevented.

‘Here he knows the mind, he knows mind-objects, and he knows the fetter that arises dependent on both. He knows how an unarisen fetter can arise, knows how an arisen fetter can be removed and how a future arising of the fetter that has been removed can be prevented.

‘In this way, in regard to the *dhammas* he abides contemplating the *dhammas* internally … externally … both internally and externally. He abides contemplating the nature of arising … of passing away … of both arising and passing away in regard to the *dhammas*. Mindfulness that ‘there are *dhammas’* is established in him to the extent necessary for bare knowledge and continuous mindfulness. And he abides independent, not clinging to anything in the world.

Bhikkhus, in this way too in regard to the *dhammas* a monk abides contemplating the *dhammas* in terms of the six internal and external sense spheres.

End of the sense spheres sub-section

Meditation Instructions

Contemplation of Dhammas [Sense Spheres]

This contemplation can be done in our daily life as well as during formal retreats by being mindful of what happens within as a variety of 'objects' [form, sound, smell. etc.] impinge upon the sense doors. One notes the feeling which arises [pleasant or unpleasant] as also any reaction [fetter], craving or aversion, which arises due to this feeling. The cause for arising of these fetters can be seen clearly in the light of the principle of dependent origination.

Thus as an example, let us consider the process of eating. We 'see' the form and colour of the food (*salāyatan paccya phassa)*, *phassa* is the coming together of the eye, the visual object and the eye-consciousness that has arisen dependent on them), it may be pleasant or unpleasant or neutral (*phassa paccaya vedanā*), and we may like it [and want to see it again] or dislike it [wish that such forms should not come before us] or just ignore it quickly. A fetter has arisen (*vedanā paccaya taṇhā*), due to mis-perception – not 'seeing' the impermanent nature of the feeling.

Now, if we mindfully observe it and neither relish it nor get angry at its arising (i.e. let it be, knowing it to be impermament) then the fetter will soon cease and further links in the dependent origination are not activated.

Otherwise, if we grasp the fetter [*taṇhā paccaya upādana*] and take it personally [thoughts like: oh! I have again become angry, etc.] it will soon blow up into a chain reaction of associated memories, expectations, (termed *papañca*, mental proliferation) and eventually some more reaction [*upādana paccya bhava*] like shouting at the person who brought the food.

Had we been very mindful, carefully noting all the links, and free from wrong-perception, we would have just noted the arising of 'seeing', followed by noting the feeling accompanying this seeing and its characteristic of impermanence. This would have stopped the chain of dependent origination right there and the feeling, instead of conditioning *taṇha*, would have strengthened our wisdom (*vedanā paccya paññyā*).

The same approach can be adapted to interaction at other sense doors. Thus when we feel the aroma of the food, if we are not mindful of the impermanent nature of feeling, whether pleasant, unpleasant or neutral, there may be a reaction – liking or disliking. We touch the food and find it too hot or too cold, and there may be a reaction. As soon as we become aware of the reaction, we prevent its further proliferation by mentally noting it and its characteristic of impermanence. We put the food in our mouth and then chew it. We may find it too hard or too slushy, and there may be a reaction. Similarly, there could be a reaction to the sound produced on chewing, the taste savoured on tongue and the process of gulping the masticated food.

At whichever level we recover the perception of impermanence, the further proliferation towards suffering halts.

Thus by careful observation we can directly 'see' that the fetters arise due to misperception of the feelings, and their arising can be prevented by cognitive training to perceive the feelings as impermanent and becoming aware of the dangers of getting attached to these.

The same exercise can be done by observing the arising of 'fetters' in others due to mis-perception, which we often attribute to them personally forgetting their conditioned nature. This often is the main cause of conflict.

Additional Remarks

Contemplation of Dhammas [Sense Spheres]

Herein an alternative paradigm of analysing whole of the subjective experience is presented, viz. in terms of the six senses and their corresponding objects and the 'fetters' which may arise in dependence on their interaction. All that happens in our life can be described in terms of these sense experiences. The objective of this contemplation remains the same as in other paradigms: to unravel the misleading sense of a substantial 'I' as an independent experiencer of sense objects, i.e. there is no 'see-er', 'hear-er', 'smell-er' etc., but only 'seeing', 'hearing', 'smelling' etc. each of which occurs when certain conditions are present.

'Seeing', for example, is possible only when there is a good eye, a visible object, light and attention. In the absence of any one of these conditions, 'seeing' can not happen. There is no independent 'see-er' waiting to see the objects as they are presented to the eye. Similarly, there exist conditions for arising of other sense – sphere consciousnesses.

The origination of mental proliferation is explained in the famous Madhupindaka Sutta (Majjhima Nikāya 18): '*Cakkhuñcāvuso, paṭicca rūpe ca uppajjati cakkhuviññāṇaṃ, tiṇṇaṃ saṅgati phasso, phassapaccayā vedanā, yaṃ vedeti taṃ sañjānāti, yaṃ sañjānāti taṃ vitakketi, yaṃ vitakketi taṃ papañceti, yaṃ papañceti tatonidānaṃ purisaṃ papañcasaññāsaṅkhā samudācaranti atītānāgatapaccuppannesu cakkhuviññeyyesu rūpesu.*

Dependent on the eye and forms, eye-consciousness arises. The meeting of the three is contact. With contact as condition there is feeling. What one feels, that one perceives. What one perceives, that one thinks about. What one thinks about, that one mentally proliferates. With what one has mentally proliferated as the source, perceptions and notions tinged by mental proliferation beset a man with respect to past, future and present forms cognizable through the eye.

http://www.accesstoinsight.org/tipitaka/mn/mn.018.than.html

The crucial stage in this sequence is the the appraisal of the feeling (*vedanā*) by perceptive ability (*saññā*) which is based on past experiences and latent tendencies dormant in the mind. Cognitive training to view the experience in the light of its fundamental characteristics like impermanence, and unsubstantialty can arrest this mental proliferation. This transforms *saññā* to anicca *saññā*, and anatta *saññā*. Girimananda Sutta [Anguttara Nikāya 10.60] points out in detail the various ways in which the *saññā* can be aligned to the true nature of all experiences.

In daily life this practice can greatly help us in improving interpersonal relationships. We recognize the arising of defilements in others due to mis-perceptions, and do not impute these personally to 'others', just as we do not ascribe the taṇhā whenever it arises within, to 'ourselves'. We know that the perception is governed by the conditions which one faces during life; it is impermanent and impersonal and liable to change through cognitive training. The resulting equanimity allows us to empathize with, rather than criticize, others. It sees the 'value' of alternative perceptions and we can arrive at a harmonious solution even in difficult situations.

Dhammas – Awakening Factors

Pali text

Dhammānupassanā bojjhaṅgapabbaṃ

'Puna caparaṃ, bhikkhave, bhikkhu dhammesu dhammānupassī viharati sattasu bojjhaṅgesu. Kathañca pana, bhikkhave, bhikkhu dhammesu dhammānupassī viharati sattasu bojjhaṅgesu?

Idha, bhikkhave, bhikkhu santaṃ vā ajjhattaṃ satisambojjhaṅgaṃ 'atthi me ajjhattaṃ satisambojjhaṅgo'ti pajānāti, asantaṃ vā ajjhattaṃ satisambojjhaṅgaṃ 'natthi me ajjhattaṃ satisambojjhaṅgo'ti pajānāti, yathā ca anuppannassa satisambojjhaṅgassa uppādo hoti tañca pajānāti, yathā ca uppannassa satisambojjhaṅgassa bhāvanāya pāripūrī hoti tañca pajānāti.

'Santaṃ vā ajjhattaṃ dhammavicayasambojjhaṅgaṃ .... asantaṃ .... 'yathā ca uppādo hoti .... bhāvanāya pāripūrī hoti tañca pajānāti.

'Santaṃ vā ajjhattaṃ vīriyasambojjh- .... asantaṃ vā ajjhattaṃ vīriyasambojjhaṅgaṃ .... yathā ca ...uppādo hoti .... bhāvanāya pāripūrī hoti tañca pajānāti.

'Santaṃ vā ajjhattaṃ pītisam-bojjhaṅgaṃ .... asantaṃ .... yathā ca .... uppādo hoti .... bhāvanāya pāripūrī hoti tañca pajānāti.

'Santaṃ vā ajjhattaṃ passaddhi sambojjhaṅgaṃ .... asantaṃ...., yathā ca .... uppādo hoti .... bhāva-nāya pāripūrī hoti tañca pajānāti.

'Santaṃ vā ajjhattaṃ samadhi sambojjhaṅgaṃ ... asantaṃ...., yathā .... uppādo hoti .... bhāvanāya pāripūrī hoti tañca pajānāti.

'Santaṃ vā ajjhattaṃ upekkhā sambojjhaṅgaṃ .... asantaṃ..., yathā ca .... uppādo .... bhāvanāya pāripūrī hoti tañca pajānāti.

'Iti ajjhattaṃ vā dhammesu dhamma- nupassī viharati, bahiddhā vā.... ajjhattabahiddhā vā. Samudayadhammānupassī .... vayadhammānupassī .... samudayavayadhamm-ānupassī vā dhammesu viharati 'atthi dhammā'ti vā panassa sati paccupaṭṭhitā hoti yāvadeva ñāṇamattāya paṭissati-mattāya anissito ca viharati, na ca kiñci loke upādiyati.

Evampi kho, bhikkhave, bhikkhu dhammesu dhammānupassī viharati sattasu bojjhaṅgesu.

Bojjhaṅgapabbaṃ niṭṭhitaṃ.

English Translation

[Dhammas – Awakening Factors]

‘Again, monks, in regard to *dhammas* a monk abides contemplating *dhammas* in terms of the seven awakening factors. And how does he in regard to the *dhammas* abide contemplating the dhammas in terms of the seven awakening factors?

‘Here if the mindfulness awakening factor is present in him, he knows ‘there is the mindfulness awakening factor in me;’ if the mindfulness awakening factor is not present in him, he knows ‘there is no mindfulness awakening factor in me;’ he knows how the unarisen mindfulness awakening factor can arise, and how the arisen mindfulness awakening factor can be perfected by development.

‘Here if the investigation of *dhammas* awakening factor is present in him, ... is not present .... how the factor can arise, and how the ... awakening factor can be perfected by development.

– ‘Here if the energy awakening factor is present in him, ... is not present ... how the factor can arise ... and how .... awakening factor can be perfected by development.

‘Here if the joy awakening factor is present in him .... is not present in him... how the ...factor can arise, and how ...the awakening factor can be perfected by development.

‘Here if the tranquillity awakening factor is present in him....is not present in him.... how the ...factor can arise, and how the .... awakening factor can be perfected by development.

'Here if the concentration awakening factor is present in him.... is not present in him... how the awakening factor can arise, and how the ... awakening factor can be perfected by development.

'Here if the equanimity awakening factor is present in him ... is not present in him.... how the factor can arise, and how the ...awakening factor can be perfected by development.

'In this way, in regard to the *dhammas* he abides contemplating the *dhammas* internally ... externally ... both internally and externally. He abides contemplating the nature of arising ... of passing away ... of both arising and passing away in regard to the *dhammas*. Mindfulness that 'there are *dhammas*' is established in him to the extent necessary for bare knowledge and continuous mindfulness. And he abides independent, not clinging to anything in the world.

Bhikkhus, in this way too in regard to the *dhammas* a monk abides contemplating the *dhammas* in terms of the seven awakening factors.

End of the awakening factors subsection

Meditation Instructions

Contemplation of Dhammas [Awakening Factors]

The awakening factors are the positive counterparts of the hindrances which arise during meditation. While the meditator works towards elimination of the hindrances, the awakening factors need to be cultivated and strengthened.

Like the earlier sections of *dhammānupassanā*, here too the practice involves becoming aware of the arising of these awakening factors during meditation. The default 'object' of contemplation could be the breath, somatic sensations, or even corpses.

When a factor is not present, one notes its absence, and when it arises one notes its presence as also the causes which help it to arise.

The conditions which help in arising of various awakening factors vary and have to be actually discerned for himself by each meditator. The commentaries indicate that some conditions are common to all the factors, viz. inclining the mind towards that awakening factor; avoiding association with people who have no inclination towards these awakening factors and associating with people who are themselves working towards cultivating them.

Other specific conditions for various factors are listed in the next section.

The set of seven factors arise progressively as the practice deepens. Thus, on the basis of well developed mindfulness, it becomes possible to investigate the nature of subjective experience. Once the investigation gains momentum, it is enthusiastically sustained with the arising of energy. This enables growth of insight, the object of contemplation becomes clearer and the meditator feels inspired to continue the practice. If at this stage the meditator doesn't get carried away by the joy arising thereof, by becoming mindful of its characteristic of impermanence, continued contemplation leads to a state of calmness, and the mind gets collected, staying effortlessly on the meditation object without distraction. With maturing insight, 'seeing' the impermanent nature of this calmness too, the meditator is established in deep equanimity.

Additional Remarks

Contemplation of Dhammas [Awakening Factors]

The commentaries indicate the conditions helpful in arising and development of various awakening factors:

Mindfulness: sustained practice and clear knowledge, careful observation to enable clear perception (*thirasaññā*)

Investigation: reflecting on the deeper aspects of dhamma; *pariyati*; balancing the five faculties; bodily cleanliness

Energy: reflecting on the fearfulness of woeful planes; seeing the benefit of effort; reflecting on the inspiring qualities of the Buddha, the *Dhamma* and the *Saṅgha*; [for monks: honoring the offerings one has received]

Joy: Recollecting one's virtues; reflecting on the Buddha, the *Dhamma*, and the *Saṅgha* and the peace of realization; reflecting on inspiring discourses

Tranquility: Comfortable posture, agreeable weather, good food; balanced behaviour

Concentration: Balancing the five faculties[3]; skill in taking up the signs of concentration; skill in restraining, inspiring, gladdening and non-interference with the mind; reflecting on the attainment of absorption; bodily cleanliness

Equanimity: Detachment towards people, things and situations, ownership of karma

The 'observation' of the presence of these awakening factors is necessary to avoid taking their conditioned arising as a 'personal' achievement which would only strengthen the ego.

---

3 The five faculties are: confidence (saddhā), energy (vīriya), mindfulness (sati), concentration (samādhi) and wisdom (paññā). There is a need for maintaining a balance between confidence and wisdom, as also between energy and concentration. This is one of the functions of sati.

Dhammas – Noble Truths

Pali text

Dhammānupassanā saccapabbaṃ

'Puna caparaṃ, bhikkhave, bhikkhu dhammesu dhammānupassī viharati catūsu ariyasaccesu. Kathañca pana, bhikkhave, bhikkhu dhammesu dhammānupassī viharati catūsu ariyasaccesu? Idha, bhikkhave, bhikkhu 'idaṃ dukkha'nti yathābhūtaṃ pajānāti, 'ayaṃ dukkhasamudayo'ti yathābhūtaṃ pajānāti, 'ayaṃ dukkhanirodho'ti yathābhūtaṃ pajānāti, 'ayaṃ dukkhanirodhagāminī paṭipadā'ti yathābhūtaṃ pajānāti.

'Iti ajjhattaṃ vā dhammesu dhamma- nupassī viharati, bahiddhā vā dhammesu dhammānupassī viharati, ajjhattabahiddhā vā dhammesu dhammānupassī viharati. Samudayadhammānupassī vā dhammesu viharati, vayadhamm-ānupassī vā dhammesu viharati, samudayavayadhamm-ānupassī vā dhammesu viharati 'atthi dhammā'ti vā panassa sati paccupaṭṭhitā hoti yāvadeva ñāṇamattāya paṭissati-mattāya anissito ca viharati, na ca kiñci loke upādiyati. Evampi kho,

bhikkhave, bhikkhu dhammesu dhammānupassī viharati catūsu ariyasaccesu.

Dhammānupassanā niṭṭhitā.

English Translation

[Dhammas – Noble Truths]

'Again, monks, in regard to *dhammas* a monk abides contemplating *dhammas* in terms of the four noble truths. And how does he in regard to the *dhammas* abide contemplating the dhammas in terms of the four noble truths?

'Here he knows as it really is,' this is *dukkha*;' he knows as it really is, 'this is the arising of *dukkha*;' he knows as it really is, 'this is the cessation of *dukkha*;' he knows as it really is, 'this is the way leading to the cessation of *dukkha*'.

'In this way, in regard to the *dhammas* he abides contemplating the *dhammas* internally ... externally ... both internally and externally. He abides contemplating the nature of arising ... of passing away ... of both arising and passing away in regard to the *dhammas*. Mindfulness that 'there are *dhammas'* is established in him to the extent necessary for bare knowledge and continuous mindfulness. And he abides independent, not clinging to anything in the world.

Bhikkhus, in this way too in regard to the *dhammas* a monk abides contemplating the *dhammas* in terms of the four noble truths.

End of section on dhammas

Meditation Instructions

Contemplation of Dhammas [Noble Truths]

This contemplation suggests viewing the subjective experience in terms of the paradigm of four noble truths.

The first noble truth suggests that all subjective experiences are unsatisfactory [*dukkha*] in view of their conditioned nature. This can be 'seen' vividly during formal meditation when *dukkha* arises as one experiences unpleasant sensations or pleasant sensations cease, mind wanders away into distressing or enjoyable thoughts etc. As in the case of other *dhamma* contemplations, the cause for the same can also be directly discerned as *taṇhā*, or non-acceptance of what is and wanting 'it' to be otherwise, i.e. some craving or aversion. Once the cause is discerned and mindfully observed as it is, without any reaction, it reveals its conditioned nature and ceases; one experiences the cessation of *dukkha*, i.e. the third noble truth. Careful contemplation reveals the whole bouquet of reasons that have really contributed to this cessation of dukkha, viz. the eightfold noble path. This is the fourth noble truth.

This contemplation can also be applied in everyday life whenever one experiences *dukkha*. Mindful observation of what *dukkha* is, (i.e. its effects on the mind and body), reveals the cause as the underlying *taṇhā*; for example, expectations [which are frustrated], or self image [which is hurt when someone criticizes] etc. This understanding in turn forms the basis for letting go of *taṇhā*. With such letting go, *dukkha* does, at least momentarily, cease. Practised in this way, one can eventually remain unruffled even amidst difficult situations.

Additional Remarks

Contemplation of Dhammas [Noble Truths]

Not only do the four noble truths constitute the conclusion of this series of contemplations, they can also be related to each of other contemplations throughout the *satipaṭṭhāna* discourse. In fact, the successful completion of any *satipaṭṭhāna* contemplation is the complete cessation of *dukkha* which corresponds to knowing the third noble truth 'as it really is'. Further, a complete understanding of the third noble truth implies a penetration of all four, since each one is but a different facet of the same central realization.

Thus the four noble truths indeed form the culmination of any successful implementation of *satipaṭṭhāna* as the direct path to the realization of Nibbāna, the complete cessation of all *dukkha*.

The term 'letting go of *taṇhā*' does not mean pushing it away, but just letting it be, without any reaction to its arising.

E. Conclusion

Pali text

'Yo hi koci, bhikkhave, ime cattāro satipaṭṭhāne evaṃ bhāveyya sattavassāni, tassa dvinnaṃ phalānaṃ aññataraṃ phalaṃ pāṭikaṅkhaṃ diṭṭheva dhamme aññā; sati vā upādisese anāgāmitā.

'Tiṭṭhantu, bhikkhave, sattavassāni. Yo hi koci, bhikkhave, ime cattāro satipaṭṭhāne evaṃ bhāveyya cha vassāni... pe... pañca vassāni... cattāri vassāni... tīṇi vassāni... dve vassāni... ekaṃ vassaṃ... tiṭṭhatu, bhikkhave, ekaṃ vassaṃ... sattamāsāni...

cha māsāni...pe... pañca māsāni... cattāri māsāni... tīṇi māsāni ... dve māsāni... ekaṃ māsaṃ... aḍḍhamāsaṃ... tiṭṭhatu, bhikkhave, aḍḍhamāso. Yo hi koci, bhikkhave, ime cattāro satipaṭṭhāne evaṃ bhāveyya sattāhaṃ, tassa dvinnaṃ phalānaṃ aññataraṃ phalaṃ pāṭikaṅkhaṃ diṭṭheva dhamme aññā; sati vā upādisese anāgāmitāti.

'Ekāyano ayaṃ, bhikkhave, maggo sattānaṃ visuddhiyā sokaparidevānaṃ samatikkamāya dukkhadomanassānaṃ

atthaṅgamāya ñāyassa adhigamāya nibbānassa sacchikiriyāya yadidaṃ cattāro satipaṭṭhānāti. Iti yaṃ taṃ vuttaṃ, idametaṃ paṭicca vutta'nti. Idamavoca bhagavā. Attamanā te bhikkhū bhagavato bhāsitaṃ abhinandunti.

Satipaṭṭhānasuttaṃ niṭṭhitaṃ.

English Translation

[E. Conclusion]

'Now, if anyone would develop these four frames of reference in this way for seven years, one of two fruits can be expected for him: either nibbana right here and now, or — if there be any remnant of clinging-sustenance — non-return.

'Let alone seven years. If anyone would develop these four frames of reference in this way for six years... five... four... three... two years... one year... seven months... six months... five... four... three... two months... one month... half a month, one of two fruits can be expected for him: either gnosis right here and now, or — if there be any remnant of clinging-sustenance — non-return.

'Let alone half a month. If anyone would develop these four frames of reference in this way for seven days, one of two fruits can be expected for him: either gnosis right here and now, or — if there be any remnant of clinging-sustenance — non-return.

‘Monks, this is the direct path for the purification of beings, for the overcoming of sorrow and lamentation, for the disappearance of *dukkha* and discontent, for the attainment of the right method, and for the realization of *Nibbāna* — namely, the four *satipaṭṭhānas.’* Thus was it said, and in reference to this was it said.

That is what the Blessed One said. Gratified, the monks delighted in the Blessed One’s words.

End

About the Author

Prof P.L. Dhar has been practising Vipassana meditation since 1985. He taught mechanical engineering in IIT Delhi for over 36 years where he also initiated discussions, and taught courses and guided projects, on interaction of Science, Technology and Human Values. These efforts resulted in setting up of National Resource Centre on Value Education in Engineering at IIT Delhi in 2001. He took voluntary retirement in 2011 to devote his time to meditation; reading, writing and lecturing on Buddha's teachings and interaction of Science, Technology and Human Values. He teaches a course on "Mindfulness- the key to inner development" at IIT Delhi and conducts 1 -day and 5-day workshops on Mindful living. He can be contacted at pldhar@yahoo.com.